This Walker book belongs to:

.........................................................

who has read this book .............. times

I've read this book ..... to ..... times

POMMY 20 30 40 50 60 80 70 70 100

I've read this book .....Basically..... times
LOADS!

Kieran

This book is worth reading
again and again... and again and
and again and
again and again and
and again and again and
again and again again and
again and again and
and again and again again

# WARNING!

This book may make you want to dance. So clear a space in your room before you begin reading

There's a quiz at the end, so pay attention to **everything**

To able bakers everywhere MT • For Alvie, Ted and Ramona BI

First published 2012 by Walker Books Ltd, 87 Vauxhall Walk, London
SE11 5HJ • 2 4 6 8 10 9 7 5 3 1 • Text © 2012 Merryn Threadgould •
Illustrations © 2012 Bruce Ingman • The right of Merryn Threadgould and
Bruce Ingman to be identified as author and illustrator respectively of this
work has been asserted by them in accordance with the Copyright, Designs
and Patents Act 1988 • This book has been typeset in Franklin Gothic and
Baskerville • Hand Lettering by Sam Pomeroy and Noah Hurst • Mouse
by Alvie Ingman and bat by Ted Ingman • Printed in China • All rights
reserved. No part of this book may be reproduced, transmitted or stored in
an information retrieval system in any form or by any means, graphic,
electronic or mechanical, including photocopying, taping and recording,
without prior written permission from the publisher • British Library
Cataloguing in Publication Data: a catalogue record for this book is available
from the British Library ISBN 978-1-4063-3157-8 • www.walker.co.uk

# RONNY ROCK starring in
# A THOUSAND TINY EXPLOSIONS!

Merryn Threadgould

illustrated by Bruce Ingman

WALKER BOOKS
AND SUBSIDIARIES
LONDON · BOSTON · SYDNEY · AUCKLAND

# 1 Ronny Rock was a very lucky boy.

It wasn't because he'd won the lottery. He wasn't a champion goal scorer. He hadn't won a talent show on TV. He didn't even have a very big bedroom.

Ronny was lucky because he lived with his dad, Mr Rock, who was a baker. And *Rock the Baker* was one of the most exciting shops in the High Street, if not the world.

As you pushed open the old wooden door of the shop a little bell rang ting-a-ling. For kids, that ting-a-ling was treacle tarts and cherry muffins. Ting-a-ling was the smell of butter, buns and bread. Ting-a-ling meant chocolate cakes for tea. Ronny would happily have spent every lucky minute of his lucky life in *Rock the Baker*.

But, like you, he had to go to school.

Ronny Rock went to St Cornstalks Primary.

St Cornstalks was a good school.

Mrs Manchet was a good teacher.

Ronny tried to be a good pupil.

But when he was meant to be doing lessons, he was most often dreaming up ideas for Fabulous Cakes and Fancy Bread.

In his history class, he invented Pyramid Bread. In English he wrote a recipe for Jam-pillows, which were like doughnuts, but jammier. And today, in science, he had come up with a really good idea for Exploding Frog Cakes.

He was busy colouring in an Exploding Frog when Mrs Manchet said she had an important announcement.

"Next Thursday is Take Your Children to Work Day," she said. "Get your parents to agree to take you to work and we can all have the day off school."

The whole class cheered.

Mrs Manchet gave out letters to take home.

And the bell rang

for break.

**2** In the playground, Ronny and his friends talked excitedly about going to work with their parents.

"My dad's job is awesome," said Scott. "He gets free tea and biscuits all day." Scott's dad was a plumber.

Abdi's dad worked on the Town Council. "I'll be on the council too," said Abdi. "Councilling."

Finn's dad didn't work, but his grandad did. Stan Flan the Lollipop Man stopped the traffic outside St Cornstalks. "I'll go to work with Grandad," said Finn, "and stop all the cars."

Gabby Bunce pointed out that no one would be at school for him to stop cars for. They would all be at work with their parents. Finn said so what, he'd stop cars anyway. And lorries.

Gabby couldn't decide whether to go to work with her mum, who was a nurse, or her dad, who was a butcher.

"What do you want to be when you grow up?" asked Ronny.

"A vet," said Gabby.

Everyone knew that Ronny would work at *Rock the Baker* with his dad.

"Will you make cakes?" Scott asked.

"Yes," said Ronny.

"Special cakes for kids?" asked Finn.

"Yes," said Ronny, "and I'm going to invent new ones."

Then everyone felt excited inside, and wished their dads owned bakeries too.

After school, Ronny was picked up by Kieran, his child-minder. Ronny liked Kieran because they laughed at the same stuff, mostly videos of monkeys burping and cats falling over.

Today Kieran had his skateboard with him. He let Ronny stand on it and he pulled him down the High Street.

"Hey, guess what! I'm getting a day off school next Thursday," said Ronny. "I'm going to work in the bakery and invent a cake."

Ronny told Kieran his Exploding Frog idea.

Kieran loved it.

"You should have different strengths," he suggested. "So a low-level Frog Cake would just shatter your teeth. And a super-strength Frog would blow your head off."

Ronny thought maybe Exploding Frog Cakes were too dangerous. He wondered what he could invent instead.

# 3

Half way down the High Street was *Ho's Newsagent*. *Ho's* stocked every kind of comic, game card, crisps and sweets you could think of. Kieran said he wanted to go in.

"Hi, boys," said Ho.

"Hi, Ho," they replied.

*Ho's* was the only place in town to sell *Paddle*, a comic about a Kung-Fu fighting ping-pong playing Duck.

Kieran loved ping-pong (he was the second best player in his school) and he was a mad *Paddle* fan, but he couldn't afford to buy it. So every month, when *Paddle* came out, Kieran went into *Ho's* and read it for free. Ho didn't seem to mind.

While Kieran was reading *Paddle*, Ronny went over to the sweet counter. There were orange drops, lemon drops, chewing gum, bubble gum, hubble gum, double-bubble-hubble gum,

gobstoppers, dip dabs and cheese lollies – all the usual stuff.

Suddenly he noticed some sweets he had never seen before. Boing Bustas, it said on the packet. Ronny bought some.

"Good choice," approved Ho as he took the money. "They made me go like a crazy man."

Ronny opened the packet. It was full of twinkly sugar dust. He shook some onto his hand and licked it.

**Suddenly ...**

# A THOUSAND TINY EXPLOSIONS PINBALLED AROUND HIS TEETH.

His hair started dancing and he turned three cartwheels.

"Boogiewoogie," he cried.

"Told you," said Ho.

Kieran was still reading *Paddle* and didn't notice anything.
Ronny bought two more packets of Boing Bustas. He had
suddenly had a brilliant idea.

**4** When they got back to the flat above *Rock the Baker*, Ronny and Kieran found Ronny's dad having a cup of tea and a bun.

"Hello, Ronny Rock Star," he said. "Good day at school?"

Ronny gave his dad the letter from Mrs Manchet.

```
Dear Mr Rock,
  Next Thursday is Take Your Children to
Work Day.
  We are asking parents to take their child
into work with them, just for one day.
  It's a fantastic idea. Your children
get to see you working hard and all the
teachers get a day off school.
  R.S.V.P.     A.S.A.P.     O.Y.B.I.T.

Mrs Manchet
```

"What a great idea," said Mr Rock. "You can see what being a baker is really like. But it means getting up very early."

"At lark's fart?" asked Ronny.

His dad said, "BEFORE lark's fart!"

"I will get up," promised Ronny. "Please, Dad!"

"The answer is yes," said Mr Rock and he signed the letter with a flourish.

Kieran suddenly remembered that he too had a letter like that.

"Oh, yeah," he said. "I'm going to work here as well, with Mum."

Mr Rock's face fell.

Kieran's mum, Tina, worked in his shop.

She could butter up old ladies, be nice to babies, keep the shop clean and add up. Mr Rock didn't think Kieran could do any of those things.

Ronny was thrilled with the news and gave Kieran a sticky high five.

They were still pretending their hands were stuck together when Mr Rock said he was off back to work.

**He told Kieran not to make a mess and not, ON PAIN OF DEATH, to finish the cheesecake in the fridge.**

The minute Mr Rock left, Kieran got the cheesecake from the fridge. He ran around the room with it, so Ronny couldn't get any.

Ronny jumped onto Kieran's back and they crashed onto the floor.

"Hey! I can do that," said Kieran. Making a shape like a starfish, he threw himself backwards towards the sofa.

Unfortunately, he missed.

# CRASH!

Tina came running up from the shop. "You sound like a couple of elephants!" she said, dragging them apart. "Stop it at once! And clean that cheesecake off the sofa."

She went back downstairs. Ronny got a cloth and Kieran turned the TV on to a rock music channel. As they watched, the lead singer of the band suddenly launched himself backwards off the stage and onto the crowd.

Tina thundered back up the stairs.

Ronny watched the rock singer get passed over the heads of the crowd. It looked like a lot of fun. He thought he would like to do that some day.

**5** The next week passed quickly and suddenly it was Take Your Children to Work Day.

Usually, on a school day, Ronny got up at half past seven. Today, his dad woke him up at half past four!

"Wakey-bakey!" said Mr Rock.

It was spooky being up so early. The High Street was dark and deserted. Ronny felt strange. He got dressed, did his teeth and put the Boing Bustas into his pocket.

Then he followed his dad downstairs and into the bakery.

**WOW!**

It was noisier and busier than he had ever seen it before.

The radio was on and the massive ovens were going full blast.

Sacks of flour and buckets of water were being kneaded into dough by giant mixers.

Racks of golden bread, fresh out of the ovens, were filling the air with a lovely smell.

Everywhere he looked, bakers were making bread, icing cakes, rolling pastry and filling tarts.

RONNY LOVED IT.

"Are you ready, son?" asked his dad. "First, we're making Cottage Loaves."

Ronny's job was to get a big ball of dough (about the size of a grapefruit) and a little ball of dough (about the size of a tangerine) and put the small one on top of the big one. Then his dad poked his finger down all the way through the middle of them both.

"That sticks the top bit of dough to the bottom bit of dough," said his dad. "And that makes a cottage loaf."

Ronny helped to make one hundred cottage loaves. Then he iced fifty-two buns and squirted cream into forty éclairs.

After that he swept up with a broom that was taller than him.

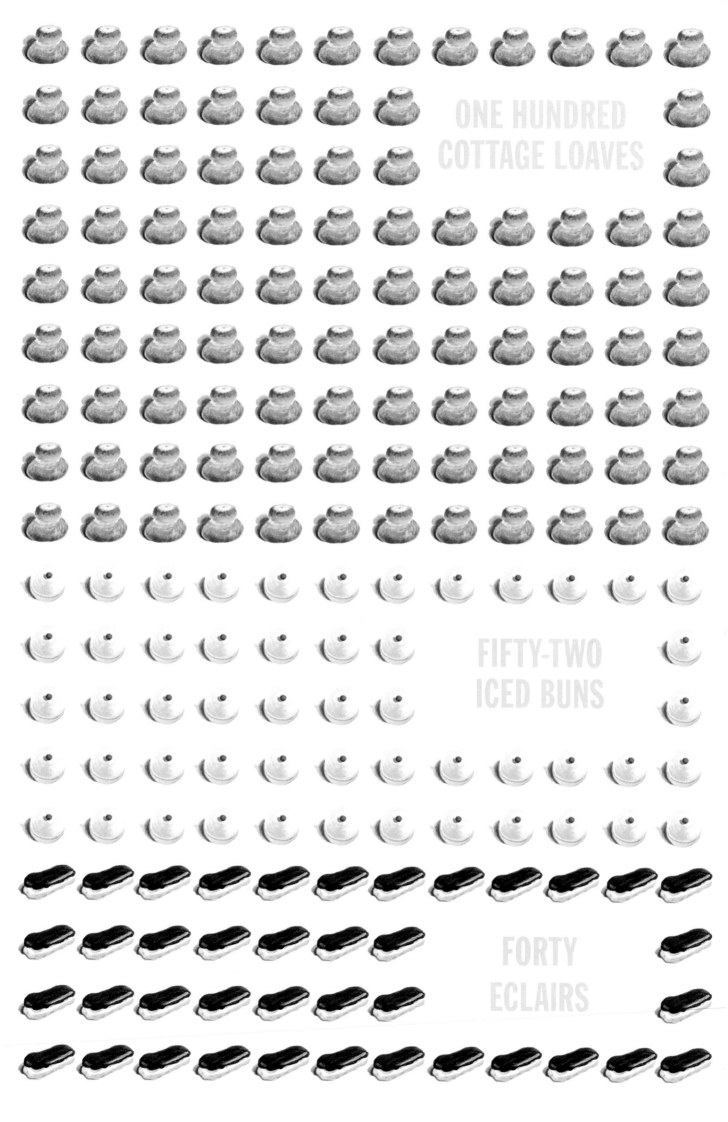

ONE HUNDRED
COTTAGE LOAVES

FIFTY-TWO
ICED BUNS

FORTY
ECLAIRS

By eight o'clock, he was tired
and very hungry.

"Time for breakfast, Mr
Baker!" said Mr Rock.

As a special treat, his dad
had made him his own tiny
Cottage Loaf. It was still
warm. Ronny thought fresh
Ronny-bread with butter and strawberry jam was the most
delicious food he'd ever tasted.

After breakfast, Ronny wanted to work on his Secret Cake idea. "Give me a call if you need me," said his dad and he went off to do other bakery things.

Ronny got some chocolate cake, some jam and cream, and the Boing Bustas and started to experiment.

By lunchtime, he'd got the ingredients right and had made ten little cakes. And that was when Kieran turned up. He had been serving in the shop all morning. Now he was on a break.

"What are these?" he asked, picking up one of the cakes and smelling it.

TEN LITTLE CAKES

"My new invention," said Ronny, proudly.

"Cool," said Kieran and stuffed one in his mouth.

Suddenly a THOUSAND TINY EXPLOSIONS zinged off his teeth. Suddenly Kieran's eyes went purple and his legs spun round like bicycle wheels.

# "Hammertime!"

he whooped, then did a back somersault
and fell to the floor like a dying fly.

Mr Rock and the other bakers came running over.

"What on earth is in those cakes, Ronny?" asked his dad.

"Boing Bustas," said Ronny. "I got them from Ho."

Kieran lay on the floor smiling. "Chillax, dude, that's awesome," he said.

Mr Rock picked up a cake and took a bite.

Suddenly a thousand tiny explosions boinged around his teeth.

"Bustamove!" he gasped and pogo-ed round the bakery.

When he recovered, Mr Rock sent Kieran to buy every packet of Boing Bustas in Ho's shop. He asked one of his bakers to make ten more sheets of chocolate sponge. Then he got out his piping gun and filled it with red icing.

"I think these need a warning," said Mr Rock. He piped a big red exclamation mark on the remaining cakes.

"Cool!" said Ronny. "And I've got a name for them …

**7** "New Today! Chocolate Suddenlys!" said the sign in the window of *Rock the Baker*.
It was half past three and there was a big queue building up in the shop. Mrs Manchet was in, wearing shorts and chatting to Ho.

Scott Dripping and his dad
were there. They were both wet.
"I fixed a real leak," shouted
Scott, waving a spanner.

Abdi was in with his dad.
They were both wearing suits
and carrying clipboards.

Finn Flan and his grandad Stan
had been stopping cars all day.

*Ting-a-ling!* It was Gabby
Bunce and her mum and
a special furry friend.

"I'm having a tea party at my house with lots of friends," yelled Gabby. "I hope you've got enough cakes."

Tina was busy with bread orders, so Kieran was serving on the cake counter.

"What are those Chocolate Suddenly thingies?" asked Scott Dripping, who was first in the queue.

"A *Rock the Baker* Exclusive, launched today," said Kieran. "Not for the under-fives or those with false teeth."

Scott wanted one. "Why are they called Chocolate Suddenlys?" he asked, as he took a bite.

Suddenly a thousand tiny explosions!

Suddenly Scott's wet hair started steaming.

"Hot Potato!" he cried and tap danced around Mr Dripping.

"We'll have two of those cakes please," said Abdi's dad. They ate them.

Suddenly two thousand tiny explosions!

Abdi and his father howled like happy wolves and moonwalked across the floor.

**"Give me three of those Suddenlys,"** ordered Mrs Manchet.

**"Two for me,"** yelled Ho.

**"Get four for us, Grandad,"** shouted Finn Flan.

**"We'll take the rest,"** screamed Gabby. Everyone grabbed cakes and stuffed them in their mouths.

# THEN THE WHOLE BAKERY WENT NUTS

Mrs Manchet began to Hula dance and Ho got a gang of builders doing the Bump.

Finn and Stan Flan began synchronized Lollipop Twirling.

Mr Dripping ate two Suddenlys together and did the Mashed Potato AND the Hokey Cokey, which got a round of applause from everyone near him.

And Gabby and all her friends lined up and did the Macarena.

People started to push in from outside and the shop bell got bored with saying *ting-a-ling.*

"Stop serving!" shouted Tina to Kieran, but he couldn't hear her through the zing and crackle of tiny explosions and everyone shouting things like "Funky Gibbon!" and "Jazz Hands!"

Ronny was laughing with delight but then Tina looked at him and mouthed, "Help!" meaning, "This is great, but soon we won't have a shop left!"

So Ronny climbed up on the cake counter and shouted for silence.

# EVERYONE SUDDENLY FROZE.

"There are enough Suddenlys to go around," said Ronny. "My dad is making loads more out the back. Please don't break the shop."

As Ronny looked down on the crowd, who were all frozen like musical statues, he remembered the rock singer he had seen on TV.

It was now or never.

Ronny turned around, stretched himself like a starfish and fell backwards. He heard everyone start cheering and a hundred hands reached up to hold him and pass him over their heads.

As Ronny got to the door Stan and Finn Flan formed
an archway with their lollipops.
"Brilliant day, eh Ronny?" asked Finn.
Ronny couldn't agree more.

## He had invented a cake that really rocked.

## He really was the LUCKIEST boy in the world.

# Explosions Quiz!

1. What is the name of Ronny's school?
2. Who is Ronny's teacher?
3. What did Ronny invent in his history class?
4. What does Gabby Bunce want to be when she grows up?
5. In Mrs Manchet's letter, what does O.Y.B.I.T. mean?
6. Who is this and what is his job?
7. What sweets does Ronny buy?
8. In Paddle, what bird does Paddle copy to give him strength?
9. What would a super-strength Frog Cake do?
10. What must Kieran not do, on pain of death?
11. How many iced buns does Ronny make?
12. Who is the first to eat one of Ronny's secret cakes?
13. What does Scott Dripping fix at work?
14. What dance is this?

# The answers

1. St Cornstalks
2. Mrs Manchet
3. Pyramid Bread
4. A vet
5. Or You'll Be In Trouble
6. Ho the newsagent
7. Boing Bustas
8. The flamingo
9. Blow your head off
10. Finish the cheesecake in the fridge
11. Fifty-two
12. Kieran
13. A real leak
14. The Macarena

# Scores

All answers right –
you win a Chocolate Suddenly!

Nine or more answers right –
you win a Jam Roll!

Less than nine answers right –
you win a Rock Bun!

life is sweet